Wicked

Aunt Baba

A Russian Tale

First published in 2011
by Wayland

Text copyright © Jillian Powell
Illustration copyright © Elena Almazova
and Vitaly Shvarov

Wayland
338 Euston Road
London NW1 3BH

Wayland Australia
Level 17/207 Kent Street
Sydney, NSW 2000

Series Editor: Louise John
Editor: Katie Woolley
Cover design: Paul Cherrill
Design: D.R.ink
Consultant: Shirley Bickler

A CIP catalogue record for this book is available from the British Library.

ISBN 9780750265355

Printed in China

Wayland is a division of Hachette Children's Books,
an Hachette UK Company

www.hachette.co.uk

Wicked
Aunt Baba
A Russian Tale

Written by Jillian Powell
Illustrated by Elena Almazova
and Vitaly Shvarov

WAYLAND

Late one afternoon, Tasha was sweeping the floor. Her stepmother watched her from a chair by the fire.

"Go and fetch some wool from your Aunt Baba," her stepmother said.

"Stepmother, I don't have time!"
cried Tasha, who had heard that
Aunt Baba was a wicked witch.

"Be quiet, child!" her stepmother said. "Here is some food to take with you."

Her stepmother gave Tasha some old meat, cheese and bread.

"Hurry! Aunt Baba is waiting," she said, pulling Tasha out of the house.

Aunt Baba lived in a hut deep in the
woods. Tasha walked through the
trees until, at last, she saw the hut.

As Tasha pushed the gate open,
it squeaked loudly.

"No one has oiled this gate in
a long time," she said.

Tasha found a can of oil nearby
and oiled the gate.

Suddenly Tasha heard a bark. She turned around to see a dog on the steps. It looked dirty and thin.

"Poor thing. No one has fed you," Tasha said.

She gave the dog the old meat and bread, and then she went inside.

Aunt Baba was waiting for Tasha in the hut.

"Come in, child," she said. "Sit down while I fetch the wool for my sister."

Baba went upstairs to get the wool.

Tasha looked around her and saw
a cat watching a mouse hole.

"Poor hungry cat," she said. "You have not been fed, either. Here is some cheese!"

The cat quickly ate the cheese and then jumped up beside her.

"What you have heard is true," the cat purred. "Go now! Baba is filling a pot to cook you in. Take the towel and comb from this table and when Baba follows you, throw them behind you."

Tasha grabbed the towel and the comb and ran out of the hut as fast as she could.

The dog was still eating the meat so it didn't bark.

The gates were oiled so they opened silently.

Soon the pot was ready and Baba came to find Tasha.

"Where are you, child?" she yelled.
"You cannot escape from me!"

Baba set off through the woods
to catch Tasha.

When Tasha saw Baba running
after her, she threw the towel down
behind her. The towel turned into
a deep wide river.

"Stupid river!" Baba roared.
"I cannot swim!"

But Baba found a boat and sailed
over the river.

"You cannot escape from me!"
she yelled.

When Tasha saw Baba climbing
out of the boat, she threw down
the comb.

The comb grew into a wood of brambles.

"Stupid brambles! Let me through!" Baba yelled.

Tasha ran all the way home. She found her father and told him all that had happened.

Her father sent her stepmother away
to live with wicked Aunt Baba.

The dog and the cat came to live with them, and Tasha and her father lived happily ever after.

31

START READING is a series of highly enjoyable books for beginner readers. **The books have been carefully graded to match the Book Bands widely used in schools.** This enables readers to be sure they choose books that match their own reading ability.

Look out for the Band colour on the book in our Start Reading logo.

The Bands are:

Pink Band 1

Red Band 2

Yellow Band 3

Blue Band 4

Green Band 5

Orange Band 6

Turquoise Band 7

Purple Band 8

Gold Band 9

START READING books can be read independently or shared with an adult. They promote the enjoyment of reading through satisfying stories supported by fun illustrations.

Jillian Powell started writing stories when she was four years old. She has written many books for children, including stories about cats, dogs, scarecrows and ghosts.

Elena Almazova and Vitaly Shvarov are an illustrator team from Moscow in Russia. Their favourite stories are those about wizards, wicked stepmothers and magical objects!